CONTENTS

Years ago, in a distant galaxy, the planet Krypton exploded. Its only survivor was a baby called Kal-El who escaped in a rocket ship. After landing on Earth, he was adopted by the Kents, a kind couple who named him Clark. The boy soon discovered he had extraordinary abilities fuelled by the yellow sun of Earth. He chose to use these powers to help others, and so he became Superman - the guardian of his new home.

THE MAN OF STEEL

DC
SUPER
HEROES

NIGHT OF A THOUSAND DOOMSDAYS

WRITTEN BY
LAURIE S. SUTTON

ILLUSTRATED BY
LUCIANO VECCHIO

COVER ILLUSTRATION BY
TIM LEVINS

SUPERMAN CREATED BY
JERRY SIEGEL AND
JOE SHUSTER
BY SPECIAL ARRANGEMENT WITH
THE JERRY SIEGEL FAMILY

RAINTREE IS AN IMPRINT OF CAPSTONE GLOBAL
LIBRARY LIMITED, A COMPANY INCORPORATED IN
ENGLAND AND WALES HAVING ITS REGISTERED
OFFICE AT 264 BANBURY ROAD, OXFORD, OX2
7DY - REGISTERED COMPANY NUMBER: 6695582

WWW.RAINTREE.CO.UK
MYORDERS@RAINTREE.CO.UK

STAR39552

ART DIRECTOR: BOB LENTZ AND BRANN GARVEY
DESIGNER: HILARY WACHOLZ

ISBN 978 1 4747 3278 9
21 20 19 18 17
10 9 8 7 6 5 4 3 2 1

BRITISH LIBRARY CATALOGUING IN PUBLICATION DATA
A FULL CATALOGUE RECORD FOR THIS BOOK IS AVAILABLE
FROM THE BRITISH LIBRARY.

PRINTED AND BOUND IN CHINA

He is...

CHAPTER 1

TARGET: EARTH

The astronauts aboard the space station were used to seeing some amazing sights in orbit. They watched the sun rise every forty-five minutes. They could view comets and stars not seen on Earth. Sometimes they even caught a glimpse of a super hero flying out of the atmosphere on the way to an interstellar mission.

But today, they witnessed something so startling that none of them would ever forget it.

A fleet of alien space ships came from behind the Moon and flew towards Earth. A normal space capsule took three days to travel that distance. The alien vessels were so fast they grew closer and closer with every minute.

"Commander! We've got company!" one of the space station crew yelled. He could not hide the concern in his voice. "Unknown spacecrafts are tracking in from the Moon."

"I have a visual," the commander said. He was on the station's observation deck. "They're coming in fast!"

"There are hundreds of them!" another astronaut said. "The radar is lighting up!"

"What's their course?" the commander asked.

"They're heading straight for us!" the astronaut at the radar post replied.

"All personnel, get to the evacuation pods!" the commander ordered. "Immediately!"

The crew of the space station scrambled to the pair of Soyuz capsules. They squeezed into the emergency space vehicles and shot away from the station.

WOOOOOOOOOOOSH!

The re-entry rockets were fired and the escape pods fled towards Earth.

Aboard the alien command ship, Queen Bloorga watched the little capsules drop into the planet's atmosphere. She debated whether or not to destroy them and the space station. She decided against it. They were worth their mass in metal.

Queen Bloorga's fleet was from a planet called Mullooska. They had used up all the water and minerals on their world, and now they were looking for more.

The fleet travelled through space searching for planets that had vast oceans and plenty of metal. Earth was perfect for their purposes.

"Captain Feg, order the fleet to surround the planet," the queen said.

"Yes, Your Supremacy," the officer replied.

The captain glided over to the control station on a smooth trail of slime. His body had the form of a two-metre snail without the shell. He wore metal armour to protect his tender flesh. On Mullooska, only the queen was allowed to have a shell.

Feg extended his long, barbed tongue and used it like a finger to operate the communications network.

BEEP! BEEP! Feg's saliva activated the buttons. He retracted his tongue. Now he could speak. "Attention all ships!" Feg said. "Form attack positions!"

The swarm of alien vessels spread out to create a ring around Earth. The ships activated their weapons. The Mullooskans were ready to take what they wanted. They were ready for a fight.

"Broadcast our demand," Queen Bloorga said to Feg.

"Yes, Your Glory," the captain replied. He pressed another button. "Attention all beings on the planet below! Surrender your water and minerals or face destruction."

The statement was short and simple. Feg had said it a hundred times to a hundred worlds. All of them had obeyed.

Feg was sure that this planet would not be any different from the others.

But he was wrong.

WOOOOOOOOOOOOOOSH! A streak of red and white flew out of the planet's atmosphere. Feg watched it on the monitors. At first, he thought the object was a missile.

"The foolish inhabitants are firing a weapon!" Feg exclaimed in surprise. "Gunners, destroy it."

KZAAAAP! KZAAAP!

Multiple energy beams streaked towards the flying target. The object dodged the beams.

"What is that?" Feg wondered aloud. He stretched his eyestalks to look at the monitor more closely.

The shape zoomed towards the command ship. Now Feg could see that the object was not a missile but a being in a white spacesuit. It had a head, two arms and two legs. Feg was familiar with beings like this. The Mullooskan fleet had conquered many of their worlds.

"Attention alien ships," a voice said over the communications network. "My name is Superman, and I protect this planet. Leave in peace."

Feg realized that the message was coming from the being in the white suit. The words did not please Queen Bloorga.

"This planet dares to oppose me?" she shouted. "Send out the troops!"

Superman floated in space outside the ship. He watched a huge hatch open in the hull of the alien vessel. The hero hoped it was an invitation to enter and meet with whoever was inside. There had been no reply on the radio that was built into his spacesuit.

Normally, the Man of Steel did not need to wear a spacesuit. He could hold his breath for long periods of time either in space or underwater. However, the hero required the suit's radio to communicate with the aliens. Unfortunately, they weren't talking.

Suddenly, a horde of soldiers in space armour poured out of the opening. They had humanoid forms, but that was the only thing familiar about them. They were not from any world Superman knew.

Their suits were outfitted with numerous energy weapons. Grenade launchers were mounted on their wrists. Flight packs on their backs propelled them through weightless space towards Superman.

"I don't like the look of this welcoming committee," Superman said.

FWOOOSH! BLAAAAM!

A grenade exploded in front of the Man of Steel. More followed. Superman evaded them using his super-speed. The soldiers tried to follow his movements but could not keep up with him.

Superman took advantage of their confusion.

ZOOOOM! ZOOOOM! He swooped in and out between the soldiers, disorientating them even further.

The soldiers turned to fire at the hero, but he was too fast. Their weapons couldn't hit him.

However, the soldiers were shooting at each other by mistake! They were caught in their own crossfire.

SWOOOOSH!

A second wave of soldiers emerged from the ship. They flew towards Superman in a huge group. They were so close together that Superman could not fly between them.

"I see they learned from their mistake," Superman said. "They're not going to let me use my trick twice in a row."

The knot of troopers hit Superman like a boulder.

KAPOWWWW!

The impact was powerful. Superman's spacesuit was amazingly strong, but the blow almost cracked it. The Man of Steel was knocked back into the upper layer of Earth's atmosphere.

Unfortunately, the swarm of soldiers came after him.

"I suppose peace talks are out of the question," Superman said. "It's time to show them that actions speak louder than words."

The Man of Steel zoomed towards the alien soldiers. He flew so fast that he was a blur to their eyes. Superman slammed into the outer edge of their formation.

KRUNCH! The impact was like a chisel hitting a rock. The soldiers were thrown in every direction.

However, the soldiers quickly re-formed and came back at him.

"You don't give up, do you?" Superman observed.

The alien soldiers flew at Superman like a swarm of angry bees. The Man of Steel met them with his fists. *POW! SMAAAAK! BAAAM!* He punched them as fast as they could come at him.

SSSMAAASH!

CRAAACK!

The force of Superman's fist broke open one of the soldiers' suits. Suddenly the alien was exposed to the vacuum of space.

Superman's first thought was to rescue the soldier. The Man of Steel had a code against killing. He was sworn to protect life, not destroy it.

Even when battling the enemy soldiers Superman hadn't used his full strength.

But now he saw the alien's face, and Superman was shocked. He recognized the alien.

It was Doomsday!

CHAPTER 2

DUPLICATE DOOMSDAYS

Doomsday was one of Superman's most powerful foes. They had fought tooth and nail when they first met. Superman lost the battle with Doomsday, but he had won the war and managed to save Earth in the process. It had taken the Man of Steel a long time to recover from the battle with Doomsday, and he was in no rush to fight the monstrous foe again.

But Doomsday was back, and Earth was in dire danger. The creature had the same powers as Superman.

Suddenly, Superman realized that Doomsday had not used any of those superpowers in this battle. He was not acting like himself at all. Whoever it was in the broken spacesuit, it couldn't be Doomsday . . .

TSSSSSSSSSS! The alien soldier suddenly dissolved. His body turned into bubbles and vanished. All that was left was the armour shell. Now Superman was certain that this was not his fearsome foe. That was a relief. It was also a mystery.

What are these alien invaders doing with a duplicate Doomsday? Superman wondered. He had a theory. Now it was time to test it.

The Man of Steel used his heat vision to slice open the armour of the nearest space soldier. Inside was Doomsday.

Superman used his hands to tear open more suits. Inside all of them were more Doomsdays. All of them dissolved after being defeated.

"They're lifeless drones," Superman realized. "Copies."

More troops assaulted the Man of Steel. They poured out of the command ship like a raging river. A thousand Doomsdays headed straight for the Man of Steel.

Superman used his X-ray vision to determine that these soldiers were not living beings. They were robots made out of organic compounds. They had no emotions. The Man of Steel did not have a code against destroying them.

Superman grabbed two soldiers and slammed them together. *SMAAAASSSH!*

As soon as the two soldiers dissolved, he crumpled the spacesuits into a ball and threw it at the other drones. It rolled through their ranks like a snowball.

ZRRRRT! Superman used his heat vision to melt their suits together.

Before long, the Man of Steel had formed a gigantic sphere of drone armour. He kicked the clump towards the empty hatch in the side of the command ship.

WHAAAM! It hit the opening and stuck there. The twin beams of his heat vision welded the mass to the hull. No more drones would come out of that ship.

"I plugged one leak, but I'm sure there are others," Superman said. When he turned around, the hero saw thousands of drones pouring out of the other alien ships.

"Looks like I've got an angry mob on my hands," Superman said.

The hordes of aliens were heading into Earth's atmosphere. The invasion force was beginning to land. There was no way to know what kind of harm they would do to the population of the planet. As far as Superman could tell, the drones were as mindless as bullets shot from a machine gun. They would destroy whatever they hit.

"It's up to me to mop up this mess," Superman said.

The Man of Steel flew at the nearest group of drones. Several thousand of them descended towards the planet. He put his hands on the chest of the soldier in front and stopped him in mid-flight. All the drones directly behind the leader had no time to stop.

BAM! BAM! BAM! Soon, there was a huge pile-up. The Man of Steel pushed with all his might and sent the mass of drones speeding towards the Moon.

In the time it took him to thwart one group of drones, thousands more were starting to enter Earth's atmosphere. Superman rocketed after them.

"I have to stop as many as I can before they reach the surface," he said. "Once they land, it will be much harder to stop them."

Even though he knew it might be dangerous, the Man of Steel took a deep breath. Then, he removed the helmet of his spacesuit and blew a blast of freeze breath at the drones. ***WOOOOOOOSH!*** It was more frigid than the vacuum of space. The drones were frozen solid in an instant.

The Man of Steel let the drones fall down through the atmosphere and burn up like shooting stars. He was already heading towards his next battle.

A horde of drones disappeared into the tops of the highest clouds. Superman used his X-ray vision to locate them. He had no trouble seeing them in the thick billows of vapour.

KRAKABOOM! KAPOW! The sound of his powerful fists hitting their armour was as loud as thunder.

ZAP! ZAP! ZAP! The flash of their energy weapons firing at Superman was as bright as lightning.

And when Superman was finished with them, a rain of broken spacesuits was falling from the clouds.

The Man of Steel searched for more enemy drones. Ahead of him, skies were clear as far as he could see. He used his telescopic vision to search for more of the soldiers.

Finally, the hero spotted a squad a hundred kilometres away and a kilometre below his position. The drones were heading for a major city. Superman recognized their target. It was his home – Metropolis!

"Things just got personal," said the Man of Steel.

WOOSH! Superman flew down through Earth's atmosphere at super-speed. The friction melted the spacesuit off his body, making him look like a meteor streaking through the sky. His invulnerable body was not harmed. The hero was called the "Man of Steel" for a reason!

As he got closer and closer to Metropolis, Superman could see that the drones were getting ready to land in the middle of the city.

Superman didn't stop. *BOOM! BOOM!* He travelled so fast that he created a deafening sonic boom.

But the sound was like a whisper compared to what happened next.

Superman took in a big breath of air that filled his lungs. Then he directed a powerful blast of frigid air at the robotic soldiers.

CRACKLE! The wave of air hit their armour like a bomb. Every metallic joint froze, then cracked and shattered. The Doomsday drones were exposed to the air of Earth. They dissolved.

Their bodies can't exist without the armour, Superman realized. *The creation process must have been a failure.*

This was a very important discovery. Now Superman knew that the drones were weaker than the real Doomsday. They had strength in numbers, but that was all.

A shadow fell over the Man of Steel. He looked up and saw another horde of enemy drones descending through the skies. The massive squadron blocked out the Sun like a giant storm cloud.

"Well, strength in numbers does have its fair share of advantages," Superman said.

ZAP ZAP ZAP!

ZAP ZAP ZAP!

The drones started firing their weapons at the city and its inhabitants.

The Man of Steel flew up and blocked the blasts with his invulnerable body.

Then he fired his heat vision in a wide arc. *ZRRRRRRRRT!* The blast scorched the armour off hundreds of the enemy drones. As one, they dissolved into bubbly foam.

BLAM!

BOOM!

KAPOW!

Suddenly, the soldiers started to explode! Superman had no idea why that was happening.

But he got his answer a second later.

FWOOOOOOOOOOOOOOSH!

Air Force jets zoomed past the Man of Steel. They fired their weapons at the invading drones.

The aircraft were destroying the drones in large groups.

The military had arrived to help Superman defend Earth!

CHAPTER 3

ALIEN TERRITORY

Army tanks rolled through the streets of Metropolis. They fired cannons at any aliens that had managed to land on the ground.

Squads of soldiers ran next to the tanks in support. The combined forces took care of the aliens that had been able to slip past Superman.

A four-star general drove an open Jeep in the middle of the action. He gripped the steering wheel in one hand and held a megaphone in the other.

General Sam Lane directed the armed forces defending Metropolis. "Team four, you missed a spot!" he shouted, hardly needing the megaphone. "Don't make me come and clean up after you!"

Superman went down to the general. He floated alongside the vehicle, waiting for a chance to talk. But General Lane did not stop. He never even slowed down.

Then Superman noticed there was a passenger in the Jeep with the general. It was a woman dressed in civilian clothes and wearing a combat helmet and vest. She talked rapidly into a tape recorder. Superman immediately recognized her.

"Lois Lane!" the Man of Steel said. "I'm not surprised to see you out here covering the story."

"You know me, I'm always on the front lines!" she replied. Lois Lane was the top reporter for the *Daily Planet* newspaper. "That's where the headlines are made!"

"I would expect no less from General Lane's daughter," the Man of Steel said.

"How about an exclusive quote for the *Daily Planet*, Superman?" Lois asked.

"I'll give you one later," Superman said. "Right now, I have vital information for the general."

The hero told General Lane that he had discovered the troops were not living beings and that they had several weaknesses. The general was glad to have the intel. With it, he could direct his forces to exploit the enemy's vulnerability.

"Just split their suits and they dissolve? We'll crack them like walnuts," the general declared. "Thanks, Superman. I'll pass that along to the other military leaders fighting this threat."

"I'm confident that the military forces around the world can handle the drones," the Man of Steel said. "The alien invasion fleet in space is another matter."

"What are you going to do?" Lois asked the Man of Steel.

"Stop them," Superman said. "And fast."

WOOOOOSSSSSSH!

The Man of Steel shot into the air like a rocket. He flew higher and higher. Soon the atmosphere thinned. Superman took a gulp of air before he entered the vacuum of space.

The invasion fleet still circled Earth.
There were no more soldiers coming from
the ships. Either they had all been sent or
some were being held in reserve for later.
Superman was determined that his adopted
planet would never see another alien
drone.

The Man of Steel turned his attention
to the command ship. It made sense that
the leader of the invasion was on that
vessel. Superman used his X-ray vision to
have a look inside. The ship was nothing
surprising, but the aliens were.

Snails? Superman thought.

The Man of Steel had travelled far and
wide in the universe. He had seen life forms
and civilizations on many planets. This one
was unfamiliar. He wanted to know more
about them.

And he wanted to know why they were trying to steal Earth's resources. So he decided to ask.

A single punch made a hole in the side of the space ship. Superman gripped the sides and pulled. **CRUNCH!** He opened the hull like a can of cat food. Then he flew through the opening and onto the bridge of the command ship.

Air rushed past the Man of Steel as it escaped through the breach. The crew was in a panic. Superman remained calm. He sealed the hole with his heat vision. Then he turned to face the invaders.

"My name is Superman, and I protect this planet," the Man of Steel said. "Who are you, and where do you come from?"

ZAP! ZAP! ZAP!

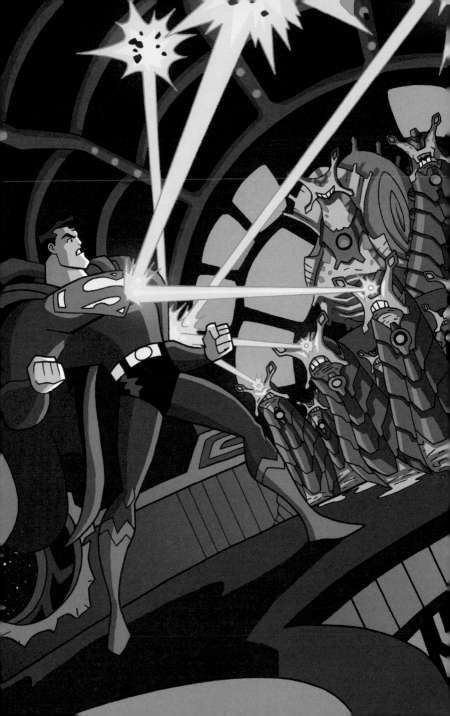

The only answer Superman got was a round of energy blasts from weapons mounted on the armour the aliens wore.

ZRRRRRRT! KA-ZAP! The beams bounced off Superman and hit the control panels, making the equipment explode.

"You might want to stop doing that," Superman suggested.

"Cease fire!" Feg yelled. He could see that this alien was very powerful. Feg obeyed power.

"Feg, are you insane? Destroy the monster!" Queen Bloorga shouted.

Superman melted all the weapons with his heat vision before anyone could start shooting again.

PLOOOOOOP! PLOP! Blobs of molten metal dripped onto the deck.

Feg looked over to the queen, awaiting orders for what to do next.

"Leave this world, and I'll let you go in peace," Superman said.

"No," Bloorga refused. "I want this planet's water and metals."

"The inhabitants need those resources," Superman told her.

"We need them more," Bloorga argued.

"You don't have to go to war for it," Superman said. "I can help you find another source."

"No. This planet is perfect, and we are already here," Queen Bloorga insisted.

"I could hurl your fleet far away from this world," the Man of Steel said. "I have the super-strength to do it."

"Then do so. It will not stop us. We will find another planet to raid," Bloorga boasted. "Will you be there to defend them, too?"

"Yes," Superman promised.

"Then I will grow more troops to fight you," the queen declared.

"Hmmm. That reminds me," Superman began. "I'm curious how you do that."

He used his X-ray vision to search the command vessel. He wanted to find out where the Doomsday drones were made. There had to be some sort of factory to create the drones.

It didn't take long to locate the facility deep inside the ship. Superman saw rows and rows of capsules. Each one held a curled-up drone.

"I see you're already busy," he said to the queen.

"My armies will be renewed," Bloorga stated proudly. "I will have your world."

"Sorry, I can't let you do that," the Man of Steel said. "Your cloning days are officially over."

Superman used his heat vision like laser beams to cut a hole in the metal deck plates. He flew through the opening and down to the next level. He punched through to the next deck, then the next and the next.

BAM! BAM! BAM! Superman worked his way down through the command ship. Soon he reached the drone factory.

Alien workers slithered out of the way as Superman blasted through the ceiling.

Superman landed in their slime trails. He hardly noticed the goo. He was too astounded by the number of drone capsules all around him. What he had seen with his X-ray vision was nothing compared to being in the actual facility.

"This looks like the lab of a mad scientist," Superman said.

"Who are you calling mad?" an irritated voice asked.

The Man of Steel looked around to find who had spoken. He did not see anyone at first. Then something moved between the rows of drone capsules.

Superman stepped closer. The thick glass of the containers warped the creature's face and shape. Six huge eyes stared back at Superman.

"You're an interesting specimen," the voice stated. "I think I'll devour your DNA!"

SLURRRRRRRRRRRP!

A long, spiked tongue stretched out towards the Man of Steel!

CHAPTER 4

THE DRONES OF KRYPTON

"Sorry, no free samples today," the Man of Steel said as he jumped away from the alien's tongue. *SLAPPPPPP!* It hit the capsule behind Superman.

The creature pulled its tongue back into its mouth and came out from behind the capsules. Superman saw that it did not really have six eyes. The goggles and glass from the capsule had simply made its head look that way. The creature was similar to the snail aliens except for the tentacles waving at its sides.

"Who are you?" Superman asked.

"My name is Gorka. I run this facility," the alien replied.

"You're the one making all of these drones?" the Man of Steel asked.

"Yes!" Gorka said proudly. "Aren't they magnificent?"

"They have their limits," Superman observed with a shrug.

"Yes, they are fragile outside of the armour," the scientist admitted. "I'm working to improve that flaw. The next batch will be fixed."

Superman knew that he had to destroy the drone factory. He could not let the invaders keep growing Doomsday drones to conquer other worlds. Not every planet had a super hero to protect it.

"I can't let you make any more drones," Superman told Gorka.

A wide beam of Superman's heat vision cut through a large section of the drone capsules. *ZRRRRRRRRT!* The slimy liquid inside boiled, then evaporated. The expansion caused the capsules to explode. There was nothing left except smoke and bubbles.

"Noooo!" Gorka screamed. "Stop!"

Superman did not stop. He advanced into the factory using his fists to break more containers. *CRASH! SMASH!* The half-formed drones plopped onto the deck. They looked more like sponges than soldiers. Then they dissolved.

Gorka watched the Man of Steel smash a path through the rows of canisters.

All his hard work was being destroyed. Then he looked down at the shattered glass. He stretched out his tongue and tasted where Superman had touched a fragment with his fist. There was a trace amount of his DNA.

"This is familiar," Gorka said. "I've tasted this DNA before. And I know just what to do with it. This will improve my drones!"

Gorka slithered away. He had to get to the central control section. He had one chance to turn this disaster into a victory.

Superman was surprised at how many drone capsules he saw. There seemed to be no end to the number of capsules in sight. No matter how many he destroyed, there were more and more after that. This did not discourage the Man of Steel.

In fact, it made him even more determined to finish the job.

SWOOOOOOOSH! A blast of his freeze breath froze a hundred capsules at once.

WHOMP! WHOMP! WHOMP! Superman stamped the ground at super-speed, causing many more to shatter.

Then he flew in circles at super-speed to create a tornado. *FWOOOOOOOOM!* It sucked in row after row of containers and pulverized them.

Superman continued to move like a circular saw through the drone factory. Then Superman stopped. The hero saw that he was in a large chamber full of electronic equipment that blinked and beeped. And there was a single capsule in the centre of the room.

The central capsule was larger than any of the other containers. It was big. And inside was Doomsday – the real one!

The Man of Steel was surprised to say the least, though he could see that Doomsday was as still as a statue inside the container. There was a bright red glow around him that served as a force field. It was the only thing that kept him from escaping.

At that moment, a pair of red and green energy beams hit one of Doomsday's spikes. *ZAP! ZAP!* A small piece was removed. The spike started to grow back immediately.

So this is how Gorka is getting the genetic material for his drones, Superman realized. *He's taking samples from Doomsday himself!*

Superman noticed that Doomsday was not totally motionless. He moved his eyes and stared at the Man of Steel. Superman could see that Doomsday was suffering tremendously.

"This isn't right," Superman said. "I don't care if Doomsday is the most destructive creature in the universe. He can't be allowed to suffer like this."

The Man of Steel clenched his fist and pulled back his arm, preparing to smash the container that held Doomsday.

ZAAATTT!

A beam of red energy hit the Man of Steel. It surrounded him, forming a force field around his body. It was the same thing that kept Doomsday in his capsule.

"Argh!" Superman groaned.

He knew this sensation all too well. "Red sun energy!" he groaned.

While the yellow rays of Earth's Sun granted the Man of Steel superpowers, light and energy from a red sun made Superman very weak.

This force field was no different. It sapped all the strength from Superman's body.

THUMP! The Man of Steel fell to his knees. He could barely move.

Gorka stepped out from behind the drone capsule. "I knew your DNA looked familiar," he said. He held the beam's control device in one of his tentacles, aiming it at Superman. "You and this creature share the same genetic structure."

It was true. Superman and Doomsday were both Kryptonian. But that was the only thing they had in common.

"Your DNA will improve my drones," Gorka told the Man of Steel. "And there's nothing you can do about it now!"

A cloning pod came down over Superman. *KA-THUNK!*

Now the super hero was trapped, just like Doomsday. A pair of red and green energy beams hit the skin on his hand.

ZRRRT! ZRRRT!

The beams burned his skin! Superman was not used to feeling such pain. He was not able to move to stop the beams or get out of the way. He was not used to being helpless, either. But that's exactly how he felt.

Those beams must be a combination of red sun energy and green Kryptonite, Superman thought. *The only two things in the universe that can hurt me.*

Every time the beams hit Doomsday his skin repaired itself instantly. That made him the perfect raw material for Gorka's experiments. Doomsday was an endless and renewable source of DNA samples.

Superman knew that Doomsday had been created as a genetic experiment.

Long ago, a cruel scientist had killed and recreated the creature over and over again. He then revived it, teaching it to grow stronger from every death it suffered.

Because of that experience, all that Doomsday had ever known was rage and destruction.

Superman did not know if there was a single intelligent thought inside Doomsday's mind anymore. He seemed to be a seething stew of anger and pain.

Superman was beginning to know what that was like. The beams burned his skin over and over, and he couldn't do anything about it. He could not move. He could not escape. He could not fight back against his captors.

The hero's frustration soon grew into anger. It was all he could feel. It was all he could think about.

"Stop!" Superman told himself. "If I can't control my anger, I won't be able to find a way out of this."

Being zapped by energy beams did not help his concentration.

Superman forced himself to focus on one thought – escape!

"Even though I can't move my whole body, I can still move parts of it," the Man of Steel realized. "I'm breathing. My chest is moving. And I can move my eyes . . ."

Superman looked over to where Gorka was growing a new batch of drones. They were starting to take shape.

And they all looked just like Superman!

CHAPTER 5

DOOMSDAY UNLEASHED!

The Superman drones grew at a very rapid rate. Cells came together to form bones and muscles and skin. It didn't take long for the first drone to emerge from its capsule.

The newly made drone stood before Gorka. The alien scientist looked closely at his newest creation.

ZAPPPP! Then he shot the drone in the chest with an energy weapon!

The drone yelled, then staggered back. The skin on its chest turned red, but the drone did not dissolve.

"Success!" Gorka exclaimed. "I've fixed the flaw in my formula."

Trapped in the cloning pod, Superman watched as more and more new drones stepped out from the growth capsules. They all marched towards rows of space armour.

Once they were sealed inside the armoured suits, they left the laboratory. Superman guessed they would be launched at Earth to continue the attack.

The Man of Steel could not let that happen.

Think, Superman told himself. *Find something you can use to escape.* Superman glanced around the lab.

Suddenly, something caught Superman's eye. He saw that Gorka had put down the control device for the force field beam. It rested on a nearby lab table.

Superman knew if he destroyed the controller, then the force field that surrounded him would shut down.

Superman could make only small movements. However, that was all he would need. While he could not move his whole head, he was able to swivel his eyes towards the control device.

Once it was within full sight, he fired the intense rays of his heat vision with every last bit of his remaining strength.

ZRRRRT! The blast was very weak and short. However, the metal device had started to melt!

TSSSSS! A tiny trail of smoke curled into the air.

SNIFF! SNIFF! "What's burning?" Gorka wondered aloud.

Suddenly, the little device exploded. *KA-ZAAAP!* The red force field switched off. Superman was free! He stood with his hands on his hips and frowned at the alien scientist.

Suddenly, Doomsday let out a fierce roar. Now that the control device was destroyed, the force field around Doomsday's prison was gone, too!

Gorka gulped. "Uh-oh," he said.

The scientist was so afraid that his tentacles began to curl up and shrink to half their normal size. He lost the strength to hold his energy weapon.

CLAAANK! The energy blaster fell to the floor.

"Drones, attack!" Gorka yelled in desperation.

The newly hatched drones turned and charged towards Superman and Doomsday. It was a weird experience for the Man of Steel. He had never before fought a foe with a face identical to his!

They had some of his powers, too.

POWWW! Two of the drones punched Superman at the same time. He went flying across the lab and smashed into a wall.

A few more of the Superman drones flew through the air towards where he landed. Superman barely managed to dodge their blows. *BOOOM! BOOOM!* Their fists made huge dents in the wall instead.

The Man of Steel was still weak from his exposure to the red rays of the force field. It would take time for him to return to full strength. Right now, he could barely manage a blast of freezing breath.

WOOOOOOOOOSH! The blast hit them, but the super drones just shook off the cold. Then they rammed Superman into a wall of equipment.

SMASH! Superman was hurt by the impact. "Unh!" the Man of Steel moaned as he slumped to the ground. The drones piled on him, swinging away.

"ROAAAARRR!" Doomsday bellowed. He grabbed the drones and threw them off of Superman.

The Man of Steel was surprised. He never expected to get help from Doomsday!

"Thanks, big guy," Superman said.

But Doomsday did not hear the Man of Steel. He was too busy smashing the super drones.

Doomsday's accelerated healing power let him recover faster than Superman. At his full strength, Doomsday ploughed his way through the cloning facility like a runaway bulldozer.

SMASH! CRASH! Doomsday grew angrier with each punch. His fury was his fuel.

Superman could not blame Doomsday for being so angry. Not this time. The Man of Steel knew exactly what the creature had suffered at the hands of the aliens and Gorka. It was enough to make a Man of Steel angry, too. And who knows how long Doomsday had been held captive.

But Superman did not let his anger control him. This was what made him different from Doomsday. This was what made him a hero.

It took only a few minutes for Doomsday to destroy the entire factory deck of the command ship. Nothing was able to stand in his way. It did not matter if the obstacle was a drone or computer. Doomsday destroyed everything. He was filled with red-hot rage.

Soon, however, there was nothing left to smash. Doomsday punched up through the ceiling and went on to the next level of the ship to continue his rampage.

Superman realized that the creature would not stop until everything was destroyed. He would crush the rest of the ship just like the drone factory.

Everything and everyone on board would be destroyed, including the strange, snail-like aliens.

"I can't let Doomsday wipe out these aliens," Superman said. "Even though they tried to invade Earth, I can't let them be killed."

Superman followed Doomsday's trail of destruction. It led straight to the command deck.

When the Man of Steel set foot on the deck, he saw that Doomsday was about to attack Queen Bloorga.

FWOOOOSH! Superman filled his lungs with air and expelled it out of his mouth as fast as he could.

The force hit everything like a hundred hammers. **_KRAKA-BOOM! ZIRRT!_** Equipment and control panels exploded. Doomsday was rocked by the gale-force blast. He was knocked away from the alien queen.

"ROARRRRRR!" Doomsday growled. He rushed back towards Bloorga.

Superman put himself between the queen and Doomsday, but even that did not stop the enraged creature. He slammed into Superman. **_KA-POWWWW!_**

More shock waves bounced around the command deck. **_CRACKLE!_** Several more control panels fizzled then exploded.

"RAW RRRR!" Doomsday howled. He balled up both his fists and hit the floor with all of his strength.

CRRRRRRRUNCH! The whole command deck collapsed underneath his fists. It fell down through all the levels that Doomsday had destroyed.

Queen Bloorga and all of her crew fell along with the falling deck. So did Superman and Doomsday.

WOOOOOOOOOSH! The Man of Steel used a puff of his super-breath to slow everyone's descent. Soon, they all landed safely. It was then that Superman realized they were back in the drone factory.

Queen Bloorga was covered by a soft heap of her crew. She stretched up her eyestalks to see where she was. She did not like what she saw. The entire facility was a charred ruin. "My drones!" she shrieked. "My factory!"

Bloorga straightened up to her full, royal height. The crew members that had protected her were thrown to the side. One of her eyestalks pointed at Superman. The other one pointed at Doomsday.

"GRRR!" Doomsday growled at her. Then he rushed towards her.

Suddenly, Doomsday bounced off a solid object. It was the Man of Steel. He stood between Doomsday and the alien queen. Doomsday howled and leaped at Bloorga once more.

WHOMP! Doomsday hit the Man of Steel again. He absorbed the painful blow.

"No," Superman said. "I won't let you hurt them."

"Grrr?" Doomsday muttered in confusion.

"These are living beings, just like you," Superman said. He wasn't sure if Doomsday really understood his words. "They were cruel to you, and to me. But they still deserve to live."

Doomsday bellowed angrily. He prepared to launch another attack on the Man of Steel.

"I saved you, but I will fight you," Superman warned. As he said it, he saw fear in Doomsday's eyes.

"GRARRRR!" Doomsday grunted. Then he punched a hole in the hull of the ship and leaped away into space.

Superman took a deep breath of oxygen, then followed out of the hole. But when he got outside, Doomsday was already gone.

"I think it's time to send these aliens on their way," Superman said to himself.

CRRRRRRREAK! The Man of Steel squeezed the hull back together with his super-strength.

Next he gathered up all the ships in the invasion fleet. *ZAP! ZAP!* He used his heat vision to melt their hulls to each other.

Soon he had assembled a gigantic ball of space ships.

The Man of Steel threw the ball towards a distant planet. He used just enough super-strength so that the ships would land safely on the surface. The world had lots of water and minerals. And that was just what the aliens said they needed.

Superman used his super-vision to look around for Doomsday one more time.

Superman could not find Doomsday anywhere. He felt relieved. There had been enough fighting for one night!

* * *

Meanwhile, Doomsday sat on an asteroid far away from Earth. For once, he was silent and still.

And for the first time in a long time, an intelligent thought had entered into his head: it was the memory of Superman saving him from the aliens.

The thought was strange to Doomsday. It made him feel something besides anger. It actually bothered the monstrous creature. It made him feel . . . good.

Doomsday lifted his hands over his head. With amazing force, he brought them down hard on the asteroid.

KAPOWWWWWWW!

The asteroid was shattered into teeny, tiny bits.

And that made Doomsday feel better!

DOOMSDAY

Real name:
Doomsday

Occupation:
Destroyer

Base:
Varies

Height:
2.7 metres

Weight:
415 kilograms

Eyes:
Red

Hair:
White

Built to be the ultimate soldier, Doomsday is unique in that he cannot be permanently killed. Each time he dies, Doomsday grows stronger – and adapts to become immune to the way he died. The more times Doomsday dies, the stronger he becomes. That fact, coupled with his cold-hearted and chaotic behaviour, makes him one of the Man of Steel's most dangerous and deadly foes.

- While Doomsday can heal himself from any kind of damage, it can take him several days to thousands of years to fully recover. The more damage Doomsday receives, the longer it takes him to return to life.

- Doomsday's body has adapted to absorb any superpowers used against him so that he can use those powers himself.

- Doomsday doesn't need to eat, drink or breathe, allowing him to survive in the vacuum of space. Those abilities, coupled with his ability to fly, means he can follow his enemies anywhere they go.

- Doomsday is covered by jagged bones over his entire body. They serve as body armour, but can also be used as slashing or cutting weapons.

BIOGRAPHIES

LAURIE S. SUTTON has read comics since she was a child. She grew up to become an editor for Marvel, DC Comics, Starblaze and Tekno Comics. She has written *Adam Strange* for DC, *Star Trek: Voyager* for Marvel, plus *Star Trek: Deep Space Nine* and *Witch Hunter* for Malibu Comics. There are long boxes of comics in her wardrobe where there should be clothes and shoes. Laurie has lived all over the world, and currently resides in Florida, USA.

LUCIANO VECCHIO was born in 1982 and currently lives in Buenos Aires, Argentina. With experience in illustration, animation and comics, his works have been published in the UK, Spain, USA, France and Argentina. Credits include *Ben 10* (DC Comics), *Cruel Thing* (Norma), *Unseen Tribe* (Zuda Comics) and *Sentinels* (Drumfish Productions).

GLOSSARY

conquered taken over by an enemy

DNA molecule that carries the genetic code that gives living things their special characteristics

drones mindless beings controlled by someone or something other than themselves

duplicates exact copies

exploit treat someone unfairly

horde large, noisy, moving crowd of people or animals

interstellar between stars, as in travelling from one star to another

invasion using armed forces to take over something

pulverized demolished or crushed completely

tremendous huge or enormous

DISCUSSION QUESTIONS

1. Who is more to blame for Superman's troubles – the snail-like aliens or the Doomsday drones? Why?

2. Do you think aliens exist? Why or why not? Discuss your answers.

3. This book has ten illustrations. Which one is your favourite? Why?

WRITING PROMPTS

1. What do you think Doomsday would have said to Superman if he could speak? Write a short conversation that might take place between Doomsday and Superman after this story ends.

2. The snail-like aliens in this story want to take over the Earth. Write a convincing short letter to them explaining why they should leave our planet the way it is.

3. Doomsday survives his encounter with Superman. What do you think Doomsday will do next? Write another chapter to this story, then draw an illustration for an exciting part of the chapter.